A NOTE ABOUT THE TEXT

The song we know today as "Over the River and Through the Wood" is adapted from a poem by Lydia Maria Child. The poem was first published in her popular three-volume anthology for boys and girls, *Flowers for Children* (1844–1846). During the nineteenth century it was reprinted many times under various titles. Child's poem became the unofficial anthem of Thanksgiving after her friend John Greenleaf Whittier included it in *Child Life* (1871), his immensely popular collection of nineteenth-century children's verse. The original poem was twelve verses long, but it has often been shortened to six. This book uses the six verses that appeared in the Whittier anthology under the title "Thanksgiving Day."

Published in the United States by North-South Books Inc., New York.
Published simultaneously in Great Britain, Canada, Australia, and New Zealand in 1993 by
North-South Books, an imprint of Nord-Süd Verlag AG, Gossau Zürich, Switzerland.
First paperback edition published in 1998

Library of Congress Cataloging-in-Publication Data
Child, Lydia Maria Francis, 1802-1880.
[Boy's Thanksgiving Day]
Over the river and through the wood ; a Thanksgiving
poem / by Lydia Maria Child; illustrated with woodcuts by Christopher Manson.
Originally published in v. 2 of the author's Flowers for children, 1884,
under the title: A boy's Thanksgiving Day.
Summary: Scenes from rural New England illustrate this familiar poem, that
became a well-known song, about a Thanksgiving Day visit to Grandmother's house.
1. Thanksgiving Day—Juvenile poetry. 2. Children's poetry, American. 3. Children's
songs—Texts. [1. Thanksgiving Day—Poetry. 2. Songs.] I. Manson, Christopher, ill.
II. Title. PS1293.B68 1993
811' .3—dc20   93-16614
A CIP catalogue record for this book is available from The British Library.

The illustrations are woodcuts painted with watercolor
Musical arrangement and typesetting by Perry Iannone
The text and display type is set in Adobe Caslon
Typography by Marc Cheshire

ISBN 1-55858-211-8 (LIBRARY BINDING)
1 3 5 7 9 LB 10 8 6 4 2
ISBN 1-55858-959-7 (PAPERBACK)
10 9 8 7 6 5 4 3

For more information about our books, and the authors and artists
who create them, visit our web site: http://www.northsouth.com

Reprinted by arrangement with North-South Books.
Printed in the U.S.A.

Over the River and Through the Wood

A Thanksgiving Poem by Lydia Maria Child

ILLUSTRATED WITH WOODCUTS BY

Christopher Manson

North-South Books

NEW YORK

Over the river and through the wood,
To Grandfather's house we go;

The horse knows the way
To carry the sleigh
Through the white and drifted snow.

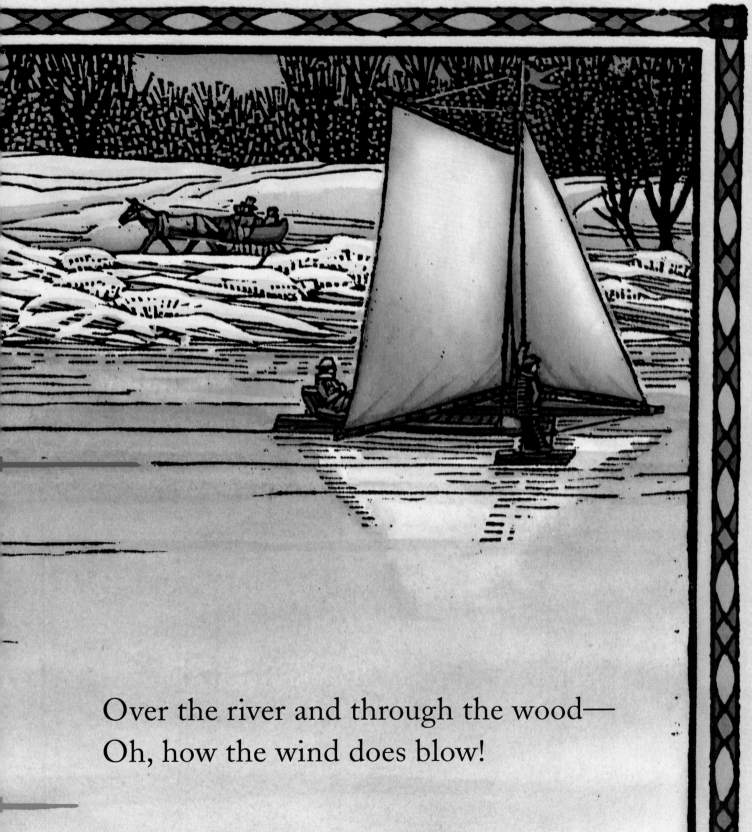

Over the river and through the wood—
Oh, how the wind does blow!

It stings the toes
And bites the nose,
As over the ground we go.

Over the river and through the wood,
To have a first-rate play.

Hear the bells ring,
"Ting-a-ling-ding!"
Hurrah for Thanksgiving Day!

Over the river and through the wood,
Trot fast, my dapple-gray!

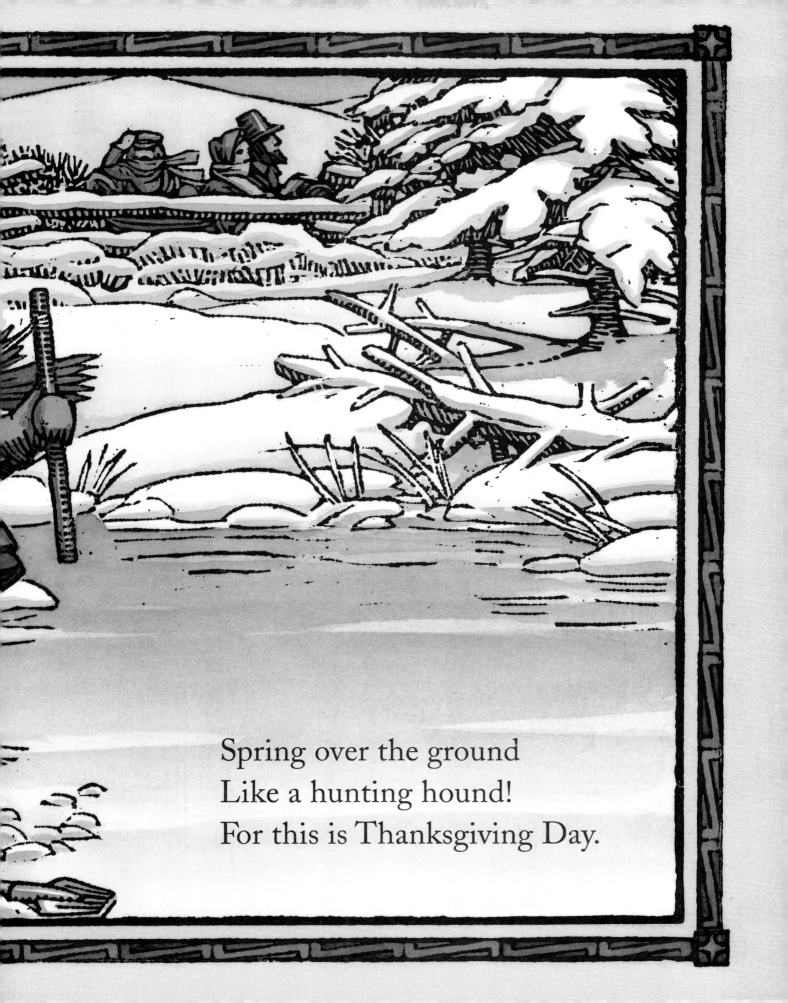

Spring over the ground
Like a hunting hound!
For this is Thanksgiving Day.

Over the river and through the wood,
And straight through the barnyard gate.

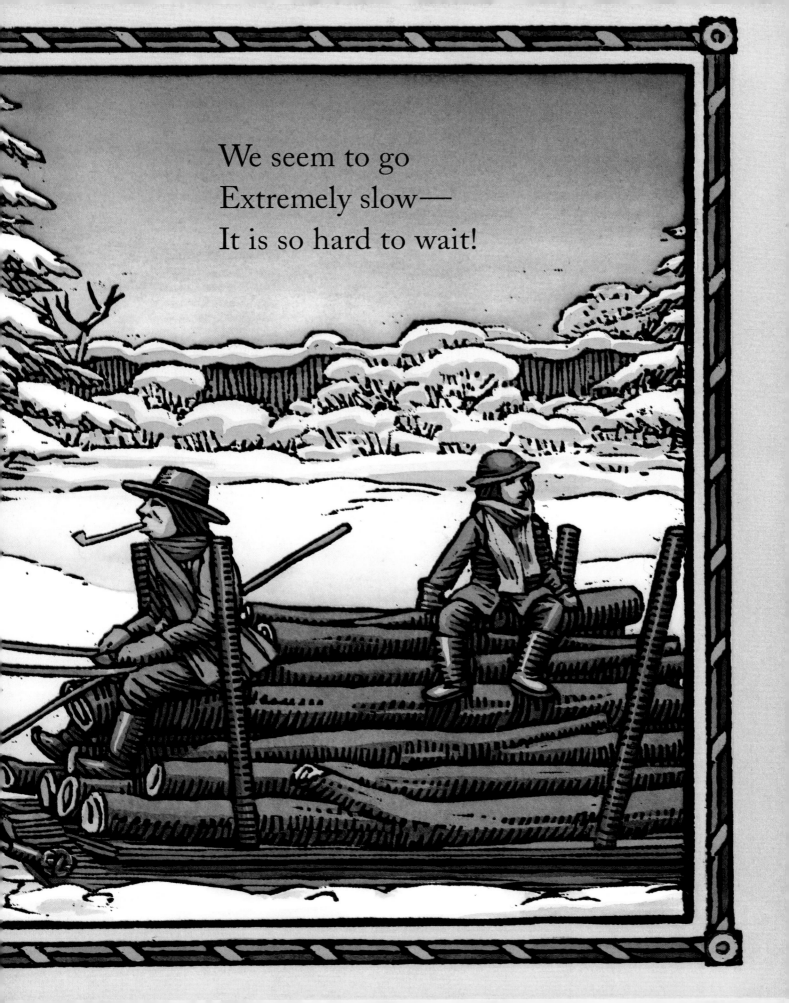

We seem to go
Extremely slow—
It is so hard to wait!

Over the river and through the wood—
Now Grandmother's cap I spy!

Hurrah for the fun!
Is the pudding done?
Hurrah for the pumpkin pie!

2. Over the river and through the wood,
   To have a first-rate play.
   Hear the bells ring, "Ting-a-ling-ding!"
   Hurrah for Thanksgiving Day!

   Over the river and through the wood,
   Trot fast, my dapple-gray!
   Spring over the ground Like a hunting hound!
   For this is Thanksgiving Day.

3. Over the river and through the wood,
   And straight through the barnyard gate.
   We seem to go— Extremely slow
   It is so hard to wait!

   Over the river and through the wood—
   Now Grandmother's cap I spy!
   Hurrah for the fun! Is the pudding done?
   Hurrah for the pumpkin pie!

A NORTH-SOUTH PAPERBACK

LYDIA MARIA CHILD (1802-1880) was a prominent nine-teenth-century American literary figure and one of the first women authors in the United States who made her living exclusively by her writing. She was an ardent anti-slavery advocate and also wrote one of the earliest feminist treatises. She was a prolific and controversial writer and produced about thirty books, including several for children.

CHRISTOPHER MANSON has written and illustrated many books for children, including *Maze, A Gift for the King, Two Travelers, The Crab Prince,* and two books published by North-South, *The Tree in the Wood* and *A Farmyard Song.*